EUROPE

ASIA

AFRICA

PACIFIC OCEAN

INDIAN OCEAN

OCEANIA

ANTARCTICA

Titles in this series

Animal Alphabet Book
Birds
Plants
Animals
Animal Homes

The publishers would like to thank the staff of World Wildlife Fund
for their help in making these books.

Acknowledgment:
The illustrations on the front and back cover, endpapers, page 4 (bottom right), and page 13
are by Stephen Lings.

LADYBIRD BOOKS, INC.
Auburn, Maine 04210 U.S.A.
© LADYBIRD BOOKS LTD 1988
Loughborough, Leicestershire, England
Panda logo © 1986 Copyright WWF – International

Printed in England

WORLD WILDLIFE FUND
Animals

written by GILLIAN DORFMAN
illustrated by PHIL WEARE

Ladybird Books

Produced in association with World Wildlife Fund

All animals breathe, eat, move, have young, and keep themselves safe and warm. What are these animals doing?

The cheetah moves across the African plains.

The squirrel eats a nut.

The seal breathes air.

The mongooses keep a lookout for enemies.

The owl feeds her young and keeps them safe and warm.

These animals are eating.
What are they eating here?

The elephant is eating
leaves and twigs.

The zebras are eating grass.

The lions are eating their kill.
The vultures wait to eat what's left over.

One monkey is eating leaves.
The other is eating birds' eggs.

These animals are hunters.
They kill other animals for food.
What makes them good hunters?

The tiger creeps up close
to its prey, then rushes
forward suddenly and grips
it with sharp teeth and claws.

The eagle has a sharp
beak and strong talons.
It can spot its prey from
far away.

The shark has strong jaws
and rows of very sharp teeth.

These animals are hunted. They are killed for food. How do they protect themselves?

The prairie dog can hide.

The antelope can run very fast.

The turtle has a hard shell that helps keep it safe from its enemies.

The sea urchin has sharp spines.

All animals need food, water, and air to live.
They get these things from their surroundings.

The water vole breathes in air from all around it.

The otter drinks water.

Their bodies use what they need and get rid of what they don't need. If they didn't get rid of *waste* they would become very ill.

This kingfisher is eating food.

The perch gets its air
from the water it swims in.

All animals can move.
Some animals fly in the air...

parrot

fruit bat

birdwing butterfly

...and some animals move through the trees.

The monkey uses its tail to grip branches as it leaps through the trees.

The sloth moves slowly. It hangs upside-down to feed.

The margay runs and jumps from tree to tree.

These animals move on land...

The roadrunner runs.

The kangaroo rat jumps.

The rattlesnake slides.

...and these animals move underground.

The worm burrows and the mole digs.

These animals move in water.

The jellyfish floats.

The shark and the other fish swim.

The turtle swims.

All animals need warmth. These animals
have fur or feathers to keep them warm.

owl

reindeer

jays

wolves

Some animals hide away when it is very cold.

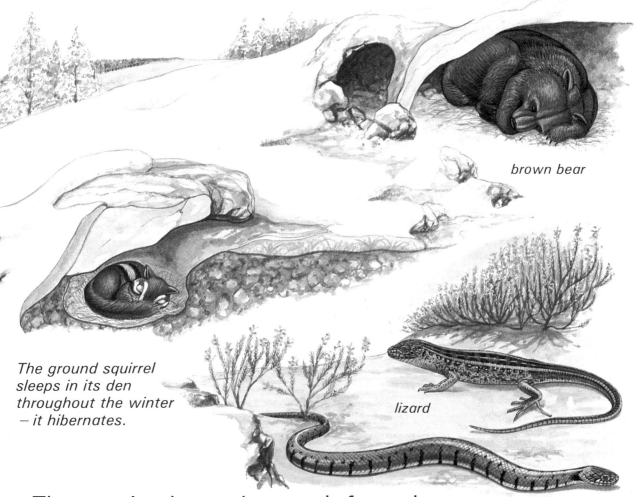

brown bear

The ground squirrel sleeps in its den throughout the winter – it hibernates.

lizard

snake

These animals need warmth from the sun so that they can move around.

All animals have young. These animals
have young by laying eggs.

Some salmon lay eggs
on the riverbed.

This butterfly
lays her eggs
underneath leaves.

These baby thrushes
are hatching from their eggs.

Some baby animals grow inside their
mother until they are ready to be born.

*A zebra foal stands up on
wobbly legs minutes after it is born.*

Here are some animal families. These baby animals look like their mother and father.

This is a fox family. The male fox is with the vixen and their cubs.

A male rabbit stands guard over a doe and her young.

Some young animals don't look like their parents.

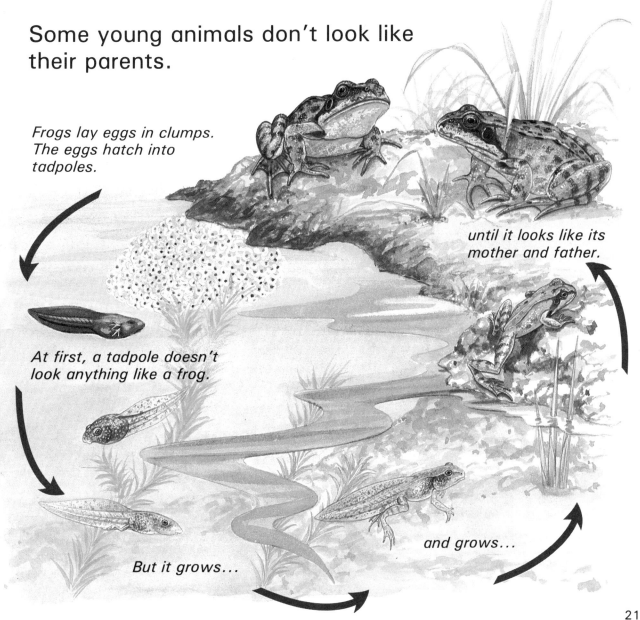

Frogs lay eggs in clumps. The eggs hatch into tadpoles.

until it looks like its mother and father.

At first, a tadpole doesn't look anything like a frog.

and grows...

But it grows...

Some young animals need help to grow up.
Their parents take care of them.

The gull feeds her babies.

The penguin guards her baby.

The cheetah shows her cubs how to hunt.

The kangaroo keeps her baby safe and warm.
The baby is called a joey.

23

Some young animals can take care of themselves.
They don't need help to grow up.

*Caterpillars hatch from eggs
and begin to eat and eat.
They don't need their butterfly
parents to help them.*

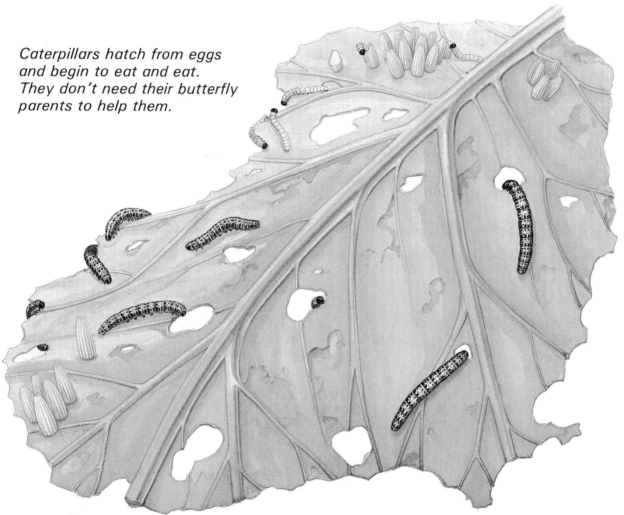

Baby turtles never know their parents.
But they **do** know that as soon as they
hatch they must hurry to the sea so
that they will be safe from enemies
like gulls or lizards.

25

There are many kinds of animals in the world. All of them use their *senses* to find out about where they live.

The fox is following a scent.

The hawk has sharp eyesight to spot its prey.

This thrush is using its sense of taste.

Every animal is special and lives in its own special way. But each one needs food, water, air, and a place to live.

If an animal has these things…it can live.

Bats cannot see very well. They use sound to find their way around.

The shrew can feel with its whiskers.

WWF

Many of our world's plants and animals
are in danger. People have destroyed or polluted the
places in which they live or grow. Some animals
have been hunted until every one of them has been
killed. This is what happened to the dodo, an
amazing flightless bird that once lived in Mauritius.
The same thing could happen to gorillas, tigers, and
whales unless we do something to save them now.

WWF (World Wildlife Fund) was set up to warn people
about the dangers threatening the earth's wildlife.
If we know and care about what happens to
our world, we may be able to protect it
before too much damage is done.

World Wildlife Fund
Membership Dept. LB89
1250 24th Street N.W.
Washington, D.C. 20037